ONLINE ACCESS INCLUDED

Professional Recordings

Favorite HYMNS
INSTRUMENTAL SOLOS

W0009183

ONLINE ACCESS INCLUDED

 To access audio, visit:
alfred.com/redeem

Enter this unique code:

00-36121_95025938

Arranged by Bill Galliford, Ethan Neuburg and Tod Edmondson

© 2010 Alfred Music
All Rights Reserved. Produced in USA.

 Alfred

ISBN-10: 0-7390-7179-3
ISBN-13: 978-0-7390-7179-3

Photograph courtesy of Barry Erra

Contents

AMAZING GRACE

TRADITIONAL AMERICAN MELODY

ALL CREATURES OF OUR GOD AND KING

DEMO 4 | PLAY-ALONG 5

By St. FRANCIS of ASSISI and
GEISTLICHE KIRCHENGESANGE, COLOGNE

HOLY, HOLY, HOLY! LORD GOD ALMIGHTY

DEMO 6 | PLAY-ALONG 7

By JOHN B. DYKES
and REGINAL HEBER

Moderately slow, flowing ♩ = 88

6

JOYFUL, JOYFUL, WE ADORE THEE

By HENRY VAN DYKE
and LUDWIG VAN BEETHOVEN

A MIGHTY FORTRESS IS OUR GOD

By MARTIN LUTHER

Majestically ♩ = 92

BE THOU MY VISION

DEMO 12 | PLAY-ALONG 13

Moderately ♩ = 104

TRADITIONAL IRISH HYMN

IT IS WELL WITH MY SOUL

By HORATIO G. SPAFFORD
and PHILIP P. BLISS

GREAT IS THY FAITHFULNESS

DEMO 16 | PLAY-ALONG 17

Music by
WILLIAM M. RUNYAN

Great Is Thy Faithfulness - 2 - 1
36121

rit.

HIS EYE IS ON THE SPARROW

DEMO **18** | PLAY-ALONG **19**

By CIVILLA D. MARTIN
and CHARLES H. GABRIEL

Gently, with expression (♩ = 108)

Verse:

His Eye Is on the Sparrow - 2 - 1
36121

HOW GREAT THOU ART

Words and Music by
STUART K. HINE

O THE DEEP, DEEP LOVE OF JESUS

DEMO **22** | PLAY-ALONG **23**

By SAMUEL TREVOR FRANCIS
and THOMAS J. WILLIAMS

Slowly and tenderly (♩. = 60)

O the Deep, Deep Love of Jesus - 2 - 1
36121

'TIS SO SWEET TO TRUST IN JESUS

DEMO 24 | **PLAY-ALONG** 25

By LOUISA M. R. STEAD
and WILLIAM J. KIRKPATRICK

Moderate folk style (♩ = 82)

PARTS OF A TRUMPET AND FINGERING CHART

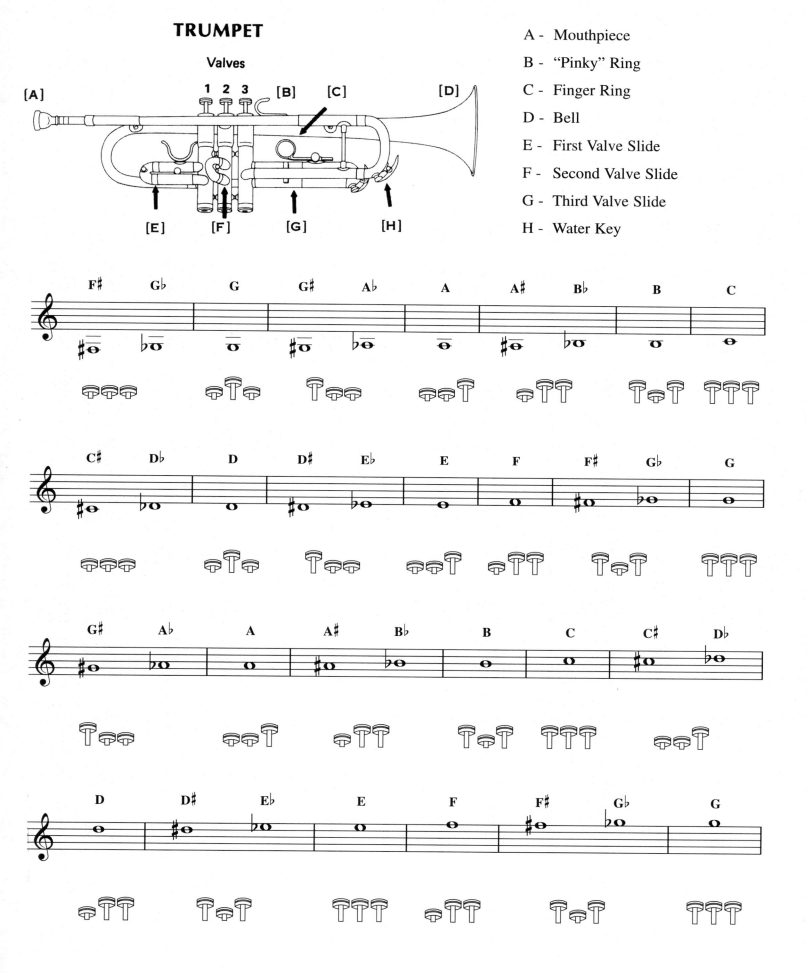